Abusing the Telephone

Abusing the Telephone

Dennis Barone

Drogue Press   New York   1994

Some of this work has appeared in *The Art of Practice* (Potes and Poets Press, 1994), *Generator, Lower Limit Speech, Talisman,* and *turbulence.*

Drogue Press
P.O. Box 1157
Cooper Station
New York, NY 10276

for Peter

Contents

Let's Play

Begin between beats, having a ball. Return to adamant female singers around blue notes' interest. Shrug out melody against strict time and formal vocalists. Jailhouse downhearted. Alternate minor distance teacher at intended rag sheet designed to play on this theme. Play on. It was cafes with dancing took people out of dreams come true. Light down below, disadvantage. All these men absent, though feeling it. Local area somber iambic sources while to return each hand usually done in voice, also. Frequency used to equal missing generation. Blue added repetition and a climax emotion. Done in narrow range, divided, dotted time to ground some fashion within each measure. Out to conform around the turn players began supporting twice the speed. Gone through several revivals, to Nebraska wound up in railroad one minute past nine. Limited elements, each one around limited themes and very systematic. Measure receives fundamental church reordering a drummer. In her voice westerns move around perfectly to wherever she wanted to be. All adds up to a powerful supplement. Yellow overlay of themes she made popular. Her art market moved in after she died. The last time I'll crawl back to you because new areas uptown liked to think tough. Define a climactic moment. I'm a ding dong use of guitar when you're smiling exactly like you. Take full responsibility then for when you're smiling so sweet. Almost all primary rules miss bottle tops swinging along a tuxedo band. Shrunken form intense voodoo in middle of good trumpet made here against tight like this syllables. A pop tune. A good man is hard to find. Revolution is not as distinct as this stuff. Now worked out drums to see traditional stuff in pessimistic masterpiece. Shrill at times, still unitary. Tiger top note, not fantasy. First to read well several records in prohibition. Shout common language toward end snare. Going this air, this fragment brushes boogie woogie solos from tea for two. Sentences: all parents musicians well adapted to the blues almost finger by finger electrically. Another case where bad conditions led to surprise paragraphs. For a short while much love. I cried for you, all the things you are. Later, this changes. A handful of keys counteracted breakfast feud. Why decline more freedom? Influence had home made reflexive. People said background killed a funny guy. Depression, swing lovers, from so rural felt understated, up tempo, puffed. Got training here in Freudian notion though critical grooving commands so much. Don't blame me, biscuit mix. The amazing, sudden trumpet now fat, developed, played. Rules lead to ecstasy. Structural inspiration not separation. Threshold. Anything else?

Everything and Nothing

I am preparing to fly. She recalls me. It is impossible to depart, history happens in rooms. Virtually all identity is fledgling. Temptation is not one stroke reorganized between excitement and failure. To recover the wariest chronicle without considering such things as the essential and permanent nature of the stone creates a predicament and open-endedness that is a poorly fitting match between a knot of thoughts and the realities of the hero.

Out of chaos and corruption my indefatigable industry is now exposed to this hot season. A moment of breath, a thought, fantasies arising out of the banality of daily life — your dark hair. My boasts are low. The pleasure in my ignorance is the joy of returning again. The pain goes, travels; it makes possible the sunlight. The reconstructed story is significant, fraught, explosive. Initiate the drama. Live, and live through that choice the way trees teach the roof to think. A cardsharp learned the first of a series of stories.

The work is remarkable, egalitarian, mature. Evidently, they refuse their choices. The *raison d'être* appears to be their homes and the chance to wear a revealing costume. A tense situation occupies him now. The excluded does not disappear but remains to disrupt the structure.

Tight enclosed spaces we don't need. What matters most questions destruction. To distinguish between fact and speculation choose truly universal topics. People saw squirrels and bears after the war. What is an agnostic?

Next time begin with the national strike. What is the significance of buildings in this book? In reality situations are never so simple. There are four kinds of audiences: hostile, impartial, friendly, and mixed. The *New Left Review* authors try to ingratiate themselves.

It was three years before it had effect. Military concerns were more important. Security demanded conformity.

Such is the case with another effort to get the self-styled formulators of public opinion to think. Inject people's minds through the medium. Combat depression, immigrants, alien sources. Thousands of reels captured and the symbols prove what the narrator tells us. There you are.

Death images replaced self-worth. Every scene broken into shots: sheep, the brain, marriage. Driven into the sea and deeply impressed, we hate the best potentialities of light. The rockiest orientations are in order. After breakfast the events lead up to New England. More rivers, and more mountains, and more towns — a thousand more.

The bright light of radiation confuses our universities. There is the idea that these men reject secret training grounds, come forth with cynicism, erase the ledgers of today. Heroes see the sacrifice of characters or attitudes provoked which challenge beliefs. Only by submerging themselves do they get the attention they crave.

Atop a hill looking down at the football field, he dies. A turning point has occurred. We see as he sees. All are rooting for the home team. Released, never introduced to this world, shot from above and lying down, longing for a secure home, framing the source of discontent, the individual must be some symbolic gesture. They were dancing for solidarity, golfing to legitimate authority. To survive, a peace must be made.

On the trip home that night, I turned to Harvey, whispering, "Just a minute." The lunchroom was empty. Just as I finished my ice cream, Billy came in and sat in one sofa before the fireplace and said furiously, "Why not me?"

Willie Masters' Niece

My head is leaking or they were always cool noses like petals of silver. It would be — my God — a smirk he'd say "unplugged." I can't for a cigarette understand a toilet lover. Departure on my own revolving, self-responsive image signifies acceptance. That's my theory.

We get used to it: bare basins and old bodies, bent and knobby. It would be agreeable, sensible to force them beautifully in and out where the sun had no skill in scripts and a wire would change to this thin sad faced guy and when you bring that balloon he grabs her and they pop.

Then there's the porcelain a violinist wouldn't trouser. I've seen that in my mouth, a sign on the stage. Now he's the crack, baldness in despair. Slowly I must be endless, white and lanky or beneath a table peering — naked, solitary, and apart. I am in the spot observant of the audience. Slowly there's other girls, but do you suppose you'd want your money back?

I said over her purchased skin: "put the horse." I plunged on, she licked her tongue with the stillness of someone who has gone away in the midst of an argument. How should I know? His breakfast table withdraws often after that language. The cardboard which just gestures signifies my see through acting.

To be careful is a reason for everything with charts. Everything else is dead. Art is the soft, crude, scorn of the machines that sound like a curtsy or a knock on a doorway panel or even eating. It's the malice I must believe for the mouth was vomiting and loving and no description can put anything into it that could be humorous. I'm only a toad in a biscuit: you can do as you please. Why, I'm my childhood blanket, a hole in my lining, licorice, the muddy circle or coffee cup. I, in fact, play the lion through just such a barrier in the book like birds you have seen under the careless side of the icon.

Who'd have thought the same soul must answer to something down the hall or stop to answer parentheses we must — with increasing indignation — think improper. Don't urge me to speak of poetry in some vast nightfall and amusement. He should say, "the gray knuckles of stone"; "life always . . . ". It's my day off. There's no looking up because when you beat me my ribs, Willie, depart both my back and the chameleon hidden in slippered feet. Conjure images and pictures, but do not say and strut when answered so luckily of language, full of liberty, *"remember."* I've an irregular tan, a grocery sticker grunting to soften blackness. I tune myself all at once in one expression you shall never know.

There is in every wheel a risk. That's how it is when we loose our tongue. Nothing was empty in the plastic bag on my chest. I know he feared his father, buttons, airmail and was born a *pro.* The photographs, the dirty ashtray, the downcast wings gesture to an actress, a shiver, a Balkan princess. In my eyes I make my mind cash like gas in a balloon, but you find particularities iridescent as a language and dangerous as new glasses.

Ruddy Duck

This endless movement which leads nowhere: a careful disorderliness is the true method. They read of truth to be found in error and consider nothing beyond the double nature of the primordial. The essence, like the man who is nothing, conceals a vulture — that heart. Before separation the letter is found to be excrement, all life stems from that matter. The cornerstone is the castaway. The carnal constitutes the true method. In some enterprises, a careful disorderliness.

Every strand of recorded existence, ancient and modern, participates in the apparently meaningful use of letters which conceal signs that have the flame of nature as emblematic in the center. Confined to North America, about 75 per cent is vegetable matter. The epistolary form invited those circles that wisdom denies and the freedom of choice, of aspiration to upward mobility is born in the mind of materialism. The balance is white with chestnut or rusty stains; the balance is blue, but less brilliant.

But never again at night justifications, ingratitude — the foundations for a land-oriented world. Of all the big overtures the rural were either floaters or oppressed enough themselves to be left outside themselves. The humiliation of sentiment predated passions with holes, according to testimony in court. A delicate fabric of self-image extended the process of holding in the fiercely devoted heart of the postwar confrontation that within their own lives directed valuable talk.

If they were both, what sort of good manners grew out of their contribution to the better standards around them? Part of the difficulty, including a strong sense of shame, is about the ways others will respond to oneself. Shame and pride underlay the prevailing standard. How rosy it all was: the nostalgia for the good old days, the recurring idea of mutual obligations.

Rarely, however, did that duty to contain defiance redefine the desperately needed, loyally rendered alternative. Most found calm performance the fate of their own hunger when the recruitment called a genesis the disintegration of the flock. (The perky, cocky manner breeds in proportion to other features.)

Of course, a vision that would gradually insinuate itself in the tendency to identify powerful assistants shouting their wildest sufferings blended into a resistance to the deepest claims of deliverance. Ill-equipped, they could not easily strengthen the expression of their models for the ostensibly unthinking and unfeeling folk of the towns simply because amusing curiosities have been seen as insurrectionary plots.

The forces of custom apparently came from the delight, affection, and love that did not suffer words like "if." It throve on an appropriate degree of respect: genuine identity. No standards, no morals. These affairs need order and fear spirited fishing with a sense of pretended childhood. Dangerous, the school cut loose a sharp line cramped, impossible to control.

The regime grew so strong by being willing to take some blows, to adjust each other in its negativity. Survival does not mean total disappearance within notes, mixed feelings, each other. A small proud bill in summer applies to both male and female. In flight, a tiny, reddish chestnut readily identified; confined.

Went. Cancelled

Another tried tourist had it with the play of circle against line. Her grown daughter, overweight, really got a kick from sleeping as if drugged. Understand that she must have been extraordinary, a stranger to the false step you share. Explain this fad, follow your footsteps; look for ways in which you laugh. He notes her dark, wet hair in the rear-view mirror.

Come on. The world is soil-to-water and desire encourages the circle that keeps talking about making. "For you." This role, stitched together, will always be separate. (Informed voice-over. Its desirability.) Copy for a friend. Why, there is no simple way, she thinks. And I pause to remember tour boats along the canal.

Joined together only to survive — constant, worn, discriminating. Worn by discriminating. Independence. Armchair, a breeze. He reversed the car and . . . and put out a restraining hand. We're supposed to drive about quietly and not to interfere. He kept his eyes closed; his head snapped back. She would have a different voice. Next door, the music school. That's what the photographers saw on his cushion back in the room. I will ask a violent man everything.

The argument went on and he stepped back to study the car. "Don't you know? He was riding a camel." It doesn't matter because we are still friends, a stretch without any side escapes, no more than a meter apart, friends. The little hairs rust eventually, but the other man stuck on the carpet's edge. The cat looked around. At about twelve he opened the door and lifted a long leg but decided to stay and pointed at the water again.

From the back of the car around eight he had noticed the wallet's absence and the traffic's flow. It is pretty clear: he is an idiot and his hand came up to hold his cheek again. I wish you good luck. The car was waiting for a green light.

19

They liked to talk of eels or, embracing her with his free arm, he'd hold up two fingers. The car moved again and the captain of the boat explained the rails carefully and repeatedly, repeatedly placed and explained. You shouldn't do that, the girl said, we agreed, but you are a man and she told him that she had removed his fingerprints. Through the soles of his shoes he had slipped into a cavity and let his hand drop back on a stack of books.

He hemmed and hawed and told me that selection is subjective. But while adding nothing to the fund of learning, he reduced to practice, with all deliberateness, statuary. We want hands, he said, too many are knocking their heads. The thing which is pointed at is this.

A pattern gives pleasure whereas eloquence is lost in contrast. February alone — or anything else — is not the pattern. If joined with prudence [the phrase is exquisite], what applauded future may their hands enjoy! (This accounts for the popularity of moral guides, wings, and ancient republics.) Yet, they rioted, coveted, despised.

It was impossible to escape. The word lives. Only through its own annihilation can it . . . The work is then the . . . The hostility felt . . . Danger. (Edited.) My creditors find precious. (Own term.) "Unfinished work." *Notes.* Plate 5. So-called. Page 7. Cannot understand. 9 x 12. Was once intended. By a similar lapse. Perspectives. Many of these other details. "Ay." Its development. Unwhiskered. Here's the boat now. It's my birthday. (As stated in the Preface.) We have left an arm unchanged; a hand, raised.

Bus Trip to Dresden

The fact that it has been considered necessary to barricade the windows with iron bars, proves sufficiently that in the course of the years important sums of money have been handled here. There is Edith. It could be Lewis standing next to her for he has been described as tall, dark, and thin. Then again Lewis's younger brother Emanuel could also fit this description. We know, too, that Emanuel wore epaulets on many formal occasions. On the back there is a signature — Edith — placed right in the spot where Edith sits on the other side. If you hold the image up to the light you can see the silhouette of Edith through the figures of her signature. This must be her signature because it matches that of the letters tied and bundled in what used to be the outer office. There is that curious looping of the first letter so distinctive of her hand as if one letter were to be stretched into two. This, perhaps, is emblem of the family's fortune. So much is owed to Edith's tenacious ability to stretch one into two. Beneath her name is the date 1895.

The year continues to puzzle me. Some of the letters indicate that Lewis had left for Japan by that year. But it is well known that Lewis often dated letters in the first month of the new year with the numerals of the prior. Hence, it is arduous indeed to reckon whether a letter dated January 1895 was actually of that year or the next. Perhaps, too, in noticing his own error he over anticipated and leapt ahead so that the letter dated 1895 might have actually been from 1894. The contents of these letters do not help much either. To establish a chronology is nearly impossible for he wrote, as he said, only of essentials. Such, nonetheless, makes the identity of the man standing next to Edith difficult to ascertain. Lewis's Japan adventures only speak against our initial summation that the tall, dark, and thin figure is Lewis. On the other hand, there is that unmistakable pose.

True, we have only read about his pose since this image is one of the few of any members of this large and prosperous family. As devout pietists they shunned pictures and publicity of any kind. This has made my work only more difficult.

Just the other day someone suggested to me that the man next to Edith might not be either Lewis or his younger brother Emanuel. This comment offered in haste caused me to consider at length my initial conjectures. If not Lewis or Emanuel, I asked myself, then who? Though this is a small detail I know that you want me to be absolutely accurate — one-hundred percent — in every detail no matter how small. And so I have thrown all other work to the side, even my planned interview with the great grandson of the stone mason who put in the bars, until such time as I can attest to the certainty of the standing figure. I am sure you would have it no other way. Accuracy, you once said to me, above all else accuracy.

It is for the above mentioned accuracy that I think it would be imprudent for me to return in haste as you suggest in order to discuss the current impasse. I feel that just a few more days here in the corporate archive will provide the necessary information to pin down at last the identity of the man who stands beside Edith. I know full well that you have certain materials in your possession that might also be enlightening in this regard, but to return and then only double back to this seems to me to be a waste of both expenses and salaried time. You must understand that as a researcher I am the paragon of thoroughness and this is exactly what I thought upon the launch of our contractual agreement you had in mind. Your family deserves no less than the services that such a paragon — and there are but few of us — can provide.

I sense that you desire something more definite, more tangible, but this is impossible until we come to the end of the matter. Then, I assure you, the whole will be made known. I have found in these investigations that one text leads to another text even at that moment of the inevitable *stumbling block*. To go on, then, leads invariably to a *cul-de-sac* and therefore at such points I prefer to go *in* rather than *on*. No doubt, there are grand questions you want to have answered and perhaps other members too have suggested possible lines of inquiry. But I must insist and persist in my insistence against loss of my situation if need be that to go *on* and not to go *in* would be foolhardy. Why, a mere ephebe could answer the questions you pose to one another at your meetings and councils. Am I right to assume that conjectures abound at such times? But who amongst you will hazard their reputation for profundity of insight by guessing the identity of the standing man? You note even here, yes, that the word we use is *in*sight not *on*sight. Hence, I'll go in or I'll go out of the whole matter and take what discoveries I have made with me to the grave!

A question for you then and enough of these requests made of me. Do you remember the exact date of the installation of the bars? Can you say something of the sums exchanged? Their amount, their purpose, the reason for secrecy and this one surviving image of the room? If secret, why have this record made of it? I see I have burdened you with something more than a single question. Whisper not a word of this to the others. I fear for your safety.

I suggest that at present you put all your energies into your planned stage adaptation of *Citizen Kane*. Fame and honor call you to the stage.

In continuing beyond this point I bother you past all bounds of patience. Nonetheless, I press on. From the top of the photograph my assistant, Jessica — you'll remember her if you recall the occasion of our first meeting. To your left and directly in back of you there sat a tall, attractive woman who had a feather in her hat. During the ensuing interview the feather repeatedly fell and she kept pushing it back up to its proper though unstable position. Out of the corner of your eye you saw this and it began, I suppose, to annoy you. Or, it annoyed you precisely because you did not exactly see it but rather saw a repeated and blurred motion — a visual fly in the ear, if you will. So, you turned and asked her if she would like to remove her hat. We all laughed. Do you remember the incident? That was Jessica.

You may regret — at this point — having hired me. True, my references were limited in number though not in quality. You will not, Sir, be disappointed. I assure you.

Let me narrate this discovery to you as the momentous event itself has unfolded before me.

"I can't read any more of this. And I won't pay for any more of this, either! Why can't he stay on one subject at a time?"

"Perhaps, he's sent us a message in code, Daddy. You know, secret symbols. It could be that important. What he says."

To hell with *Kane*. I must tell you what I've been thinking. An ORIGINAL idea. Forget about your photograph for once. I may not have gotten to the bottom of it, but I have found out who the Quaker Oats man is. That's not, though, what I want to tell you today. What I want to tell you will save you. You'll make a fortune four times as large as the Colorado Load, a hundred times. This is a dynamite idea. I call it: The Moving Picture Show Man.

Here's the gist of the story. You supply the music. A handsome young man travels to small mid-western towns in the 1890s to show films. In Centerville his equipment breaks. He falls in love with the local beauty queen who always wanted to get out of town and be a star on Broadway. They stay in Centerville and open a movie theatre.

Hotdog, this'll make you a million dollars. We can begin in the town, not out of it. Think of the saving this'll represent in set costs.

I remember my uncle in *The Rainmaker* (the Hapsfield Players version) and how he performed the whole thing with his fists clenched. Will have none of that of course.

I look forward to hearing from you.

Onward,

"We just can't abandon him. It could be true."

"He shouldn't be in Italy anyway. I'm not paying for someone's vacation. I want information."

"You could use the phonebook."

"Funny, very funny."

"But, Daddy, he could be in trouble. We've got to do something."

"What do you suggest I do. He's up against the entire Mafia, Sweetheart. Our hands are tied. Tracing those last few transactions was a goose chase. We all knew that. And now he's become the chased."

"They'll kill him."

"Save me some money, then."

"Aren't we responsible since we hired him."

"We hired him to answer some question in our past. He's got tangled up in his own. That's no sweat off our necks."

"What if he has the answer?"

"He'll wire."

"What if they get to him first?"

"We'll send someone else to pick up the pieces of the puzzle right where he left them."

I don't have much time. They're everywhere. Seems some ancestor of mine had an estate here that fell into a

Mafia family's hands some time ago, but I am — legally — the rightful heir and they think I'm here to claim my property. Madness. This might make the best spectacle. Though when it's real and happening to you it no longer seems the stuff of fiction.

I've found the stamp. I don't know how much further I'll get. They're everywhere. Suggestions? I want nothing to do with this property. I'm a genealogist. I told them. That only made things worse. The narrowness of these streets has given me my only protection. Why isn't anyone talking about table-top fusion anymore?

"O.K. It's like this. Everyone's been guaranteed 2,000 extra dollars to teach a course on Ethics. At the last moment the administration refuses to pay. What's the faculty to do? You see, we just can't abandon him in the narrow sea-side streets of Naples. Employers also have obligations. That's why I've decided to go there myself. Now, I can go either with or without your blessing, Daddy. Why don't you send me off with it."

"I can't, Sweets. It's a dangerous place. Just last Sunday the Travel Section ran an essay on pickpockets and you don't speak the language. Besides, I know what usually happens in these rescues. Love follows. There's no room for it. We've got a company to run. Don't you think these are the obligations of which you should be thinking? Besides, you'll remember what happened in *Brideshead*. Charles went all the way to Morocco to help Sebastian and he didn't even want his help."

"Oh, Daddy. Why does everything have to be so complicated? Can't some things be simple. Sometimes I get up and look at my shoes and ask the metaphysical question: why left over right? Did you ever think of it? I mean, why left over right? Why not right over left? And by the time

28

I'm done tying my shoes, I'm exhausted. Wiped out. Ready for bed again."

Whipped up. Who was I? For me it was enough. I had to make myself absent in order to be present there. Paris. Customs. My head in the sand. For me it was enough. But after dinner, fresh despair. I preferred not to see them, opened the door to go, but could not bring myself to do so. Atmospheric pressure and no bright colors. I am sure. As for the agony, no one could have understood my feelings at that moment. I felt that I should. Anguish, anguish through love. Many years passed. It seemed a long time since. Never again will such be — but her dress, her eyes, her lips. I should never have had her and so it is within our past — a labor in vain, futile. Suddenly the memory returns. I have only the narrowness of the streets to protect me. She led. Rosy candlelight color of late spring. Fragrant air. Embalmed. She did not always. I would go in and kiss her. When up is written many times on a single line it begins to look like down. This is why I could not understand why she said to use the food processor. A web, then, not the sense of center, but of what it's made. Do not move to the center, but to the side where the words are like "equal" and "divide." Black long legs. Brown body. Red under throat. Long yellow bill. Strange sharp, short call.

"I must go to him."

"You're overstepping employer-employee relations. Profits for people and profits for industry are often contradictory. Mind you, listen to what I say, if you leave now you'll never get so much as a farthing from me again."

"So the photographic image is a double image."

"What one learns from history, my dear, is that problems separated by time are better treated as separate problems and not as similar ones. Take the following as example: Atomic research in the 1930s and 1940s may have been similar to DNA research in the 1960s and 1970s, but the surrounding characteristics of the decades within which the controversy of such research evolved were vastly different. Bomb research was a centralized war time effort whereas recombinant DNA research was a local and diffuse peace time effort. Those who spoke for a moratorium on the latter were way outside the limits of their expertise. My point then is that you too don't know what you're talking about. History doesn't repeat."

"Ah, ha! That's precisely the reason I must go to him. The probability that we've unleashed a dangerous agent is real and there is no way to test for the danger. You have told me so many times, that the scientist does not know what he has done until he has analyzed the newly created — at which point it may be too late. It's our only chance. I've got to take it."

"True, risk taking is inherit in all technique, but my sense is that you're more interested in synthesis than analysis."

"I am not wearing glasses and on the verge of letting my hair down. Come on! It's more than matching green ink to green ink or fighting Trask. The whole way the factories are busy. Where is our business?"

The eighteenth-century is longer than the twentieth yet George Bellows is now an antique and no longer a modernist. A man drowning in the troubled waters a small twig may support for a few moments, but the next surge that comes will beat him off. Here he now lies; his lips, sealed, will never warm, invite, or persuade you anymore.

A deformed Florence gave form to space. We wandered into a dark alley, made fools of ourselves, broke the peace, and tempted the watchman. We walked erect and yet were not the form of human beings, for we were one mass of rags and sores, pollution and disease. The earthworm went crawling over one fellow's brow. A child ought to have no ears or eyes, but as a parent directs for a bystander often sees more of the game than those who play. Oh, strengthen my arm in the cause of sensorious world! What a horror, this game.

The sky is obscured by driving clouds. A misty rain is falling, and the wind howls in gusts. Shall I outlive the sets of my own battlements? If so, by wits alone. My gloomy edifice, one story in height, rises like an evil thing in the moonlit air. What if the candle goes out and leaves me in darkness and with the dead hand upon my knee? I digress, but even in my digression the suspense is compelling. Grief is a tree that only has tears for fruit.

I begin with the sense of adventure that I felt after I embarked on my rescue. Few will share it. I have neither the time nor the space to explain it fully. And my love, that too is beyond explanation. Maybe if I could tell you with some accuracy about the car or the umbrella, even what was in the bag. I am not an expert and I have only memory.

I am, like my father, better with the philosophical musing than with the close attention to detail. What use to describe the car? There was no car. No rain, no rain and no umbrella. There was only the gun and my reluctance to use it.

Times have changed and a lot of beans have been spilt. Everyone is busy, defeated, but not alone. There are no porters on the trains out of Chicago. Anything you do deeply is lonely. I have looked for a single image. It became a mirage. Yet, it is true: a camel goes days without water.

A man in a trench coat. A cord around the back of his neck. What else could I think? He was not my love; he was my enemy. But I am getting too close to the details. What's philosophic in a cord? I will record the event perhaps. I will never recall it. History is the vacuum that runs this machine that I call night and you call the Republic.

I've never seen him in an ascot. I've always seen him in turtlenecks. In Trenton — where it began — in Dresden — where it would end — turtlenecks. He spent his whole life in them. He doesn't so much wear the turtlenecks as stuffs them with the being that he calls himself. His whole life in front of cameras. His wife is dead. Took the secret behind the shell with her. He hides his doom. Why is it that James Dean died? Some people use the toenails of turtles to tell fortunes.

Once I thought I knew with certainty the effects of my actions. Daddy made fun of me. Where is that certainty now that the revolver has been emptied of its thought? Once I thought I knew his name.

He has on his blue sport coat. He talks. He is on his way. I follow. He has on a blue sport coat and a turtleneck. He talks. He is in a car, on his way to an opening. He sits in the back of the car. This is my report. He has on a blue sport coat and a turtle neck. He is in a car, speaking and not driving it. The servant drives the car. Images can be deceiving. They arrive.

"You don't get it, do you?" I said to Daddy. "There's a civil war in my mind." Did I fire the weapon to free or imprison myself? I may have surrendered all in my action against one. The philosophic is my strength. Since childhood: Socrates to Sartre. Ssh, no details and no confusion.

He moved fast and certain. In that respect, too, he resembled Bond. The big difference is that Bond worked for the government whereas he worked for himself. People loved him. He must have rescued half of California from extinction. Few knew about this. On occasion he could be tough skinned and hard-shelled. More often, he was a soft-hearted gentleman of the old school.

That car and the bag and a man in a trench coat with his umbrella opened even though there was no rain. Each night I see it. First, the headlights and then that exaggerated wave. I only hear the gun. Funny that I never see it. Each night when I see the car and the umbrella and the man holding it and I hear the gun, each night I look inside the bag and the bag is empty. I wasn't supposed to see that. Any of it. I know I'm through. A goner. Daddy, oh, Daddy, I'm through.

We began with a sentence and somewhere in the sentence was an idea. To awaken out of the soporific past found walking still in the present we said we would begin. So by May we had it. But there we were, stuck. In some bizarre arrangement a storehouse rich and full and at some necessary moment, emptied of its holds. Take the line as necessity rather than as trope or figure. The next read something about the nature of all art and the need for some community.

So, this guy comes to the town, you see. And he's got all this equipment, you see, for the projection of movies. But then when he gets into the town something breaks. He's sold tickets already. But no show. You see? So, the people are pretty upset. Ready to kill, almost. Except one, nice girl. She wants to go to Broadway, be a star. So, you see, they're copacetic from the start. Anyway, the industry changes, the couple falls in love, they stay in town, open the mid-west's largest theatre chain, and, as they say, live happily ever after.

One was followed by another and another. The next one had a letter that set some things straight. The community again, to attempt at least some gesture. The long wave as indication of the possible. There was no need to say what was already deed stronger than word alone. Two shots. A change in format. I do not shutter. I do not smile before the shutter. Each of us does what we must do. The question is to keep doing it, not to relinquish the inheritance. Two shots. I relinquish nothing, but use this moment to accept my responsibility.

The first and last good thing he said was that the sound of the sirens reminded him of the *Jeopardy* theme song. Turtleneck and sport coat. Sport coat and turtleneck. The yard stick fails the same as any measure. Mathematics in such situations disappoints us. Poetry, too, turns to gibberish. I feel like Margaret Fuller fast approaching the falls and saying I can't remember. The hyacinth boy used the yardstick to beat us. The mist of words has blinded all my thoughts. My train of thought become now a chain.

"I can't talk long."

"Where are you?"

"In Italy. I'm leaving for Germany."

"Why? Where in Italy?"

"Naples. Because I need a vacation. I've got to get out of here. My head is on fire."

"Slow down. What's wrong?"

"Everything."

"The rescue mission?"

"A failure."

"Why?"

"Why. Because things aren't as they seem."

"I hear you, my child. But if they aren't as they seem, then how are they?"

"Terrible. Terrible and horrible. I can't talk now. My bus. I've got to go. There's no point . . . "

"What? There's no point in what?"

"Not now. I'll call again when I get into Germany. Long ride. Long, but nice. The scenery, at least. So long. Bye."

What do they do in tropical countries to keep envelopes from sticking closed too soon? The Book contains the first word into which all other words fit. People have gone mad trying to spell it. Its letters formed in the scale of a human body at a ratio of ten to one and each letter is in a grid of one-hundred squares. Put your best foot forward. Even in its blackness the sky does not rest. My days become too muddy for sparks.

So many thoughts crowd the first that what seemed brilliant in the original fades in all that follows. The subsequent extinguishes the gleam of the pristine first. On the other hand, I heard a person from the West, perhaps in her late twenties, proclaim to her friends in the hotel bar: "Germany will lead the way and the rest of Europe will follow!" Mine is the blood the mellow grape contains: an atom of an atom-world at most.

I have an idea I must cable. Use pornography to teach illiterate men how to read and use recipes to teach women. All is not as it seems. A fortnight more and I linger no more. The answer awaits. Hence, I go.

In Dresden the chorus of the finest gymnasium accompanied by a newly uniformed marching band will be singing ever so sweetly Springsteen's "Born to Run" as they open the doors of the new Kimpinski Hotel where once for decades stood the ruined palace as a reminder of World War and other horrors. This I got to see. I don't mean to preach, but I was there when it was Dr. Zoom and the Sonic Booms and now it's an international language, "a suicide rap, a death trap. We gotta get out of here while were young because . . . " and you know the rest.

Remain calm. I couldn't decide at first. He had strange ways of doing things. He would finish a task and then come to me pleading. His habits were strange and unusual.

His first day he spent arguing over money. I was outside the office photocopying a dummy corporate yearbook. I listened closely to his argument. He moved his hands slightly as he spoke. Daddy didn't find out until weeks later that I had been outside listening the whole time. He sat with his hands clasped motionless upon his desk top.

We went for a walk. He was so thin and vulnerable. Lacking all common sense, he would have been thrilled if we embraced right there in the chapel. I couldn't. I didn't — not then, not yet.

He had an office across the hall from my studio. It wasn't really an office. A small bed served as a couch. We sat on it and he placed his hand on my leg as we spoke. I wasn't surprised.

"Would you like to get undressed," I suggested.

"It is hot," was all he said and that did surprise me. He took his hand off my leg. But then he tried to unbutton the top of my blouse and I had to yell at him.

"Take off your skirt," he said. The sunlight filtered through the half closed blinds.

"Why not just lift it up," I said. Couldn't he get it from my tone what I really meant?

"I can't get it off myself," I said, "too many buttons and other gadgets, so why not just reach up my thighs and rip it off?"

I pushed him away, but he thought my push was my way of saying "yes, yes." He told me later that he thought I wanted to control everything, that I liked it that way. We got off to a bad start, but then again there should never have been a start and now here I am remembering this long after — so it seems — the finish.

I leaped forward and kicked him. He stroked his wound with the hand that he had previously had on my leg.

"Why did you do that," he said.

"Get you out of dreamland," I said.

He had a freckle near his nose. I found myself concentrating on that freckle and then I realized that my fingernails were digging into the palms of my hands.

He rested on the couch made out of a bed. For a moment. He asked, "What was that?"

"Good," I said and I straightened my skirt and I was warm in the summer heat and I was good.

He said my name, stretched a hand out to me. Slowly. He wanted to touch me again. I could not. The sprinkler had been turned on and the plants outside got their water; the soil, its water. Through the half-drawn shades I saw this as I turned away from him. I saw the water and the plants and the soil. Can I live without him? I turned and saw that he had crawled toward me.

"Slow down," I said.

"I can't," he replied.

And then I looked out the window, through the half-drawn blinds again. He fell then to one side and moaned as if he'd hurt himself. I looked at him. His face all red, but then he laughed and the skin changed back to flesh tone, but his breathing didn't slow or quiet because he laughed so hard he nearly choked.

"Look outside," I said. "There's a brand new bright red fire engine."

I had a dream the day after I saw him practicing his serve in the gym. I had not forgotten. He was fashionably thin. I loved that. I bit my lip with my teeth. I loved to watch him. His gaze reached me. He wrapped a coat of fire around us. I could not move. My body was stiff. He stood still and stared at me. Then I was alone; my vision blurry. He appeared as if in a thick fog, but a moment later very clear and distinct, a slide moving in and out of focus in a slide projector. Tears fell from my eyes, saliva rolled out of the corner of my mouth. I heard the corniest jazz music in the background. His red mouth, his empty eyes, his naked body moved closer to me. Slowly, he extended his hand. The coat of fire moved as he moved. "Take my hand," he said. I stared at those hollow eye sockets. Meanwhile the corny jazz music continued. At this moment it was as if I recognized who he was for the first time. A voice shouted, "One, two, three" and the music changed, got faster. I never dreamed he was this evil. He drew his gaze away from me and dragged it over his body. I followed. He tried to tempt me. I wanted to. I knew I could not. I didn't want to touch him. I knew I could not. "Come," he said. I wouldn't move, couldn't. It was a dream. No big deal anyway. I stood still and stared. A voice yelled out "One, two, three" and the music and the dream stopped.

I watched him serve. He caught my eye for a moment. Why was I there? My whole body felt like a weight and to that was a chain and he held it, controlled me as he lead me by it and he knew it.

So it began. We went to my room. No one went to my room, except me. We went to my room. It was a large room; barren, but large. Very arty and loft-like, though it wasn't a loft. It was a room in the house. I turned the radio on, one of the few things in the room besides a clock, a bed, an old alligator suitcase, open. I went to him after he had taken off his socks and sneakers. We started to dance, he snapped out a rhythm with two fingers. Our feet moved around and around the room. Decorated just right for dancing I thought. Toe tapping, finger snapping fast dancing. He'd lift me up and put me down. Did this over and over. He laughed.

"We belong together, don't we," he asked.

"Yes," I said. "Yes." We bounced up and down like a couple of toys, a couple of pogo sticks.

"Are you good in math," he asked.

"No."

"Good."

And we spun around and around in my barren, arty, loft-like room to no music but the sound of snapping fingers and pounding feet. I was happier than I had ever been in my life. No regrets. Lucky, I thought. I was very, very lucky. Bless all. I felt fine. He turned over, turned over again, and got out of bed.

He buttoned his shirt. Button by button. He pulled his collar closed and made a false shiver. He stood there a moment. His shoulders were square and strong. They did not have the scholar's slouch. His hands moved to his hips and he shook his head a little, side to side, and then a little more. He leaned forward. I saw him then suspended in space for a moment up so close. I kissed him. He stepped a step away from me. It seemed forever. He turned and left singing a silly song: "Sweet lovers love the spring. The spring time. Hey ding-a-ling-a-ling. Sweet lovers love the spring."

We didn't see each other for some days after that. I felt an incredible sadness. Then I called his office from my studio. Silly, all this in the same house. And I said, "Come over here." He did. I could write here about shirts, standing, sitting, falling, but won't. Outside a fire engine siren howled in delight.

I wrote poems. What strange desire. Desire is strange. I thought: at least a little unusual. Now I have taken the poems, crumpled them into little balls, and tossed them one by one into the Elbe. I cannot bear it. I picked it up and felt it hard and cold in my hand. One shot. That's all. That's all that they needed. Little boys. The poems could have been a hymnal or at least the start of one. Prayers offered to the God of infatuation. Some of me has fallen out the window, into the Elbe on the wings of those words I stood ready once to offer as proof or tokens of my love.

One morning, the next morning, the morning in the middle of the next week — I'm not too sure — there was a note pinned to the door of my studio.

> The page is black and white,
> the road is long and black.
> Put some oil in a pan,
> send smoke signals if you can.

So he had left, hot on the trail of the mystery of the hand in the frame. Two weeks went by. I could feel that nothing was going right. His first communication said: "Pleasure only comes to the man who shows himself humble. I try to buy girls drinks. No one will let me."

We didn't know what it meant. Was he held captive somewhere? Was he telling me to date others, as they say? Was he telling Daddy to take his mystery and his money and shove them, as they say? (This "as they say" I picked up when recently reading *The Collected Prose of Robert Creeley*.) When the second communication came — a cassette tape of renaissance flute music — another possibility struck us: he's gone crazy.

General "keeping up" became a chore for me. I would loiter here and there throughout the day. I would turn to the "People" section of every paper and read the whole thing. I looked at ads: soap ads, stocking ads, jewelry. This became habit and this became pleasure and work and my life as I had known it became a chore.

One day in a bookstore I had a crisis — a near crisis. I so needed a gospel truth, a text from him that could be understood. A doctrine to continue by even if just "I ate. I slept. I ate." I started to look through the books in the bookstore for a message from him. Then I worried that someone would see me when finally I found one. What if the cashier sees me sweating, hears me breathing? I worried. Everywhere I looked I only saw stories or rather just words from violent stories. "Man dead." "Two knifed." "Bomb explodes killing baby." Do boys have these problems I wondered? I heard dogs barking outside and thought that they barked at me. Could I disguise my guilt? What guilt? I bought two magazines: my shame and guilt, violent filled. At home I stared at their narratives of guns and gangs and crimes. No message therein. My crisis now and what would I do?

I decided to waste no time, to reach for the top, the most powerful, the CEO. He played tennis. I knew that. Didn't they all? Edith had kept a Bible on top of her racket when not in use — blessed. I watched Daddy from a discrete distance and as I watched I planned. I planned a scheme not to make the organization mine, but to make me more a part of the organization. The times-they-are-a-changing.

Two weeks went by. The mechanism had been started. The cause in play and I awaited the effect. The summer was almost over. It was now or never. I had forgot it was summer. Strange that I should forget. On Friday my notice went up. The order, the length, the vocabulary are all unimportant. There was a drift to it and like Neptune and the sea I was behind the drift of it.

The next afternoon I disguised my voice and phoned him. I knew no one else would be home and he would believe it. My hero. I would receive the pleasure without any of the guilt. He would say over and over again, "how foolish of me. I'm so stupid. I can't believe it." At four o'clock prompt the messenger was at his door as we had arranged by phone two hours before.

I, of course, had stolen the photograph. I knew how much he treasured it; how much he puzzled over it. He would take it out of its box, look at it, put it back, take it out, over and over again.

He answered the door. I watched from a distance. No one else was home. I knew that. My messenger said that she had found it near the path in the woods that leads to the courts. He believed her. My messenger was beautiful and he said he wanted to reward her. He stepped inside for a moment and then returned with a beautiful bracelet that he placed on her slender wrist. I am no authority on these matters. He did not let go of her wrist. She said thank you and he said it is my pleasure. Still holding her wrist in his hands he looked up to her eyes and told her that their meeting meant more to him than the image. He softly touched the top of her blouse with one hand while he still held her wrist with the other. I was surprised. I was shocked though I don't know why I should have been. I moved away from the doorway in which I had secluded myself.

Then I heard him say it: "We're all alone. Do you think she could have taken it? I knew that only you would have found it. I know."

"I can't," my messenger said.

"I don't want you to," Daddy said.

"But I shouldn't," she said.

"Why not?" he asked.

"Don't question me," she said.

Then he pulled her close into his arms, embraced her, and started to kiss her. Just then — on impulse — I came out of the doorway, walked right up to them, and said "Smile when you talk about me." It was all I could think of to say. What could I do? I had no reason left either. Just desire, strange desire that left me only with instinct, instinct that led to impulse. But then I weakened: my power flame extinguished, but not yet my heat.

42

I had the permanent desire of art and not that temporary sort of fashion, of flings. I would rescue him. I didn't know what to do. I was unsure. I was unsure about what to do. Meanwhile, she had pushed me aside, breathing heavy. "I did what I was told," she said and added, "I'm keeping the bracelet." This is the sentimental — the strap that beats us. She to one side and I to the other. She towards the wall and I towards the door. We were both breathing heavy. "Go ahead," he said, "rescue him just like Edith rescued Emanuel."

I hugged him then. I was on top of the world. She was crying, confused. In my dreams she shoots me right after I shoot him, adding a third shot to the first two fired. All this time it wasn't a fire engine at all. It was the law.

The wound wasn't nearly so bad as it looked and to me it wasn't nearly as bad as that first wound. They've got nothing but time here. Back home time ended a long, long time ago. I'll heal here, heal well here. Beneath a bridge, in a park, by the side of the road. Who will care about one refugee from the future, from the end of time. I'll send them my identification card. One last time, I'll send it. They'll know.

"To be square again, not whole which is round, but cornered in the present. To turn back again into the past and to go pass all the houses. We lived in all of them. Here is the house of our waking. By the ferry sits the house of our dreaming. Here is our newest bomb, dense stellar corpse of our being. Tongue tomorrow and it too turns into yesterday. To be square again, not full which is solid, but emptied into a pocket turned inside out. Where we are, we are. Gasses suck us from a neighboring star. We whirl. The whirl winds us around at a quarter of light's speed. We are shrinking, yet gaining weight. We say 'next,' but it sounds like 'last.' The bright light that pulsed at the automotive plant rushed us to a corner and out under the line to disappear beyond one of the corners, to go out under the line into emptiness, past the present moment of our turning and into the instant undreamt. Some things bind us, others pull us. So many things depend upon and depend ever deepens. Woman crusades to save dogs from escalators. Let the end be complete when the last sentence is understood. The carver carves; I sing. Shall I speak: then let my words be stone. God died at dawn. There wasn't room for both of us. We had the same spirit. Spunk. The calendar closes as the day begins. My signature: Say Cheese."

As soon as I heard them introduce the ambassador I knew that I had to leave. There had been too much gunfire already that evening. I would not add anymore to it with volleys both verbal and other. On my way out someone grabbed me by my arm and pulled me into a dark room. It happened so fast. By the time I realized what was going on, it was too late to react in any effectual manner. The door slammed shut; the lock turned and clicked.

I learned much later that the ambassador had been ordering these secret abductions for over six months. Many had disappeared this way. I am sure this is what happened to many people we read about in the newspaper. And now to me! Yet, even now I regard the ambassador as my very dear friend.

The food riots had occurred just over a year ago. Some of the larger countries could have easily solved this problem, but they all followed the leadership of the largest which believed the outcome of one nation's struggle uncertain and so did nothing. Many of the poor died in these riots. How many? I do not know; one is too many.

There in that darkened room my mind wandered. What do I know? I am not poor and never will be. Without a cent to my name — even then — I could not be counted among the poor by the census takers.

I crawled in the dark toward where I thought there might be a fireplace. Where else to look for a secret passage? I found the fireplace and smiled. This was too easy. It seemed like a scene from one of the films that play in theatres and distract the minds and dissipate the energies of the people. I reached up and felt a globe of cold metal. I began to pull myself slightly and then noticed that it was loose. Of course, this was it. But did I turn the orb clockwise or counter-clockwise? If I turned it the wrong way would the room begin to shrink until it pressed me to death or would poisonous gas stream out of the fireplace and they'd find me the next morning my hand still locked on the cold metal orb? I turned it. Which way I cannot remember. Perhaps it would only turn one way. There was no gas, no diminution of the room. As the secret door opened the room seemed to expand a thousand fold. There in a brightly lit room much larger than seemed possible were many of the people who had disappeared.

I entered the bright light of the room, left the darkness behind me. The secret door closed with the loud sound of antiquated gears slowly turning, but no one turned and looked at me. They kept on typing. I walked toward one, almost bumping into others as they typed trance-like in that white, brightly lit room. These were people I had seen out in that other world before they had disappeared. I recognized some of them. They were oblivious to me. I had to dodge a few as I moved or else I would have knocked into them as they walked unshakable in their seemingly pre-ordained paths.

I looked at what one of them was typing. There was a list of women's names, some I recognized. Then he started to type some paragraphs that I couldn't quite make sense of at first. Something like this:

It is certain that in key areas, although they will experience it, they will hesitate to move into our

45

future. They have not yet categorized points. They will require conflict in the factors crucial for the basic topic. Product: the present divisions. Lift skirt, get ride.

This so reminded me of one of his messages that I tried then to grab the typist and pull him toward the labyrinth as earlier that night I had been pulled toward the dark. I could not move him. He would not stop typing. No one in the light would stop doing anything. I pretended I was the whistle of a train and then the explosion of a bomb. Nothing. I took a pencil from the desk, turned, and went off to enter the labyrinth beneath the old section of the city. With the pencil I drew a map so that others could follow.

At the station there was only one bus and Dresden was its destination. I boarded. Slept. Got here and took a room on this river boat turned into a hotel. It sits still, locked to the bank, amidst the rapid current of this wide river. I sit, part of this Canaletto view, and write what I remember, trying to figure out what it all means.

No luck. Try again. "Why see one? The advocates. Hex to some whole. Sin for the advocates tenfold. Add the sin to the hex that one sees. Why divide the whole? Test not and remain one. Question and part the one, now no longer whole. Advocate the position of sin in the side of why and then there is no divide.

This, then, being accomplished, brings us back to the very first transaction in the equation that commenced our study of the education suitable for today's world of rapid change and steady growth. Repeat the above."

"Must be code. Symbolism at least."

"No, Daddy. Believe me. He's dead."

"But Sweets, I keep getting messages from him."

"They may be in code. I'm not sure. But I am sure they're not from him. "

"They must be."

"They're not. Believe me. I know."

"How do you know? What do you know? Tell me."

"Not now. Next time."

"They sure look like they're from him."

"I know where they're coming from and they're not coming from him."

"From where then?"

"You wouldn't believe me if I told you, Daddy. You wouldn't believe me."

Persistence. "There once was a town. On Fridays serpents reigned. All the casting for the play had been completed long ago. What began as an outline became a border. Mother couldn't believe it. Little has changed.

After the war was over we returned at night to the parking lot. I'm glad we both brought chairs. The bus arrives early in the morning. These smallest things are the quickest to be forgotten. Newspapers print too many stories. That's what history teaches us. You have been a student of architecture. All the streets are strewn with leaves.

Experience the corridor where there is no corridor. Experience the light now that there is no light. Experience the corridor where there is no experience. The angel has been slain. This has been our history."

The day mechanically fell together, insisting upon itself in the same way that clocks mark the progression of time. My notes here. From my room in the floating boat hotel. "Everything is connected out of ignorance. All my certainties . . . but, but the moment you accept it, the present is inescapable; a camera, no longer. I used to think that I would have to reject the other, a pure and luminous gesture. Wake up! Human behavior makes no sense. The force of

47

revelation, literary symbols. I wanted to tell him that I'd hit bottom. I realized that there were no simple solutions. His motives were quite different, no more than a charade. He was a symptom of my ignorance; a growing obsession. Maybe I could start just one idea of my own, fill in gaps, solve life's mysteries. Considering the attitude of the French hierarchy in matters of this kind, there can be little room for doubt."

It seemed that for so long no one was listening, except for a few people, but of course I want the people to hear who aren't hearing, who aren't seeing. He helped an awful lot. He listened, encouraged, criticized, always with compassion and understanding. It is difficult to explain the emotions of love relationships, but he made me feel like a woman. I have courage now, confidence, competence, and I grew in that love. Grew to understand myself. I love him, loved him. I do not mean to sound romantic about this, the most extraordinary, the most singular, the most unexplainable part of my life. It is a love that brought to my life happiness and courage and wisdom.

The people kept shouting for Hamp's "Flying Home," and finally he did it. I can now believe the story I'd heard in Boston about this number — that once in the Apollo, Hamp's "Flying Home" had made some reefer smoker in the second balcony believe he could fly, so he tried — and jumped — and broke his leg, an event later immortalized in song when Earl Hines wrote a hit tune called "Second Balcony Jump."

The traffic on the Elbe was once considerable. So they tell me. The few unofficial people who are around to tell one anything. The once dense population of the Saxon plain seems to have dispersed sometime before my arrival. I have heard much of the new Kimpinski hotel, but have seen no construction. The restoration of the Palace at Pillnitz continues while all else around it decays. Florence on the Elbe does the "Second Balcony Jump." It was not my best choice. But all the buses came here, here opened at last; yet with no one at home.

As a trafficker in climaxes and thrills and characterization and wonderful dialogue and suspense and confrontations, I have outlined the Dresden story many times. Perseverance. "This hieroglyph. The rose. The cat. The first. The other. Not captured, constructed. How avoid it? A rhetorical question. A day, adrift. The sky sweats and grows hugely: scan the opus sans last things, etc. The word alone will not suffice. Interrupt its silence. If it is a secret, then to speak it is to commit to it. Our words are stone to its paper. I sing. Who is ready for that? The patron gathers stones. Don't we expect the sculptor to cut the stone? More than please us, the words police us. You can't know the start until you discover the end.

A vegetable guilt encyclopedia of chants. A mercantile pewter bird. A wooden image B-movie duck. A fly off theatrical tum tum soap cakes. Drama stops empty words contingent to origin. Teeth shelter principles of design. The object takes material possibility as unsure measure.

Interiors around walls last only so long. Move the door off by violence. By violence unhinge it. The organic cloakwork chooses self-distrust and the surface disguises nothing more flammable or less messed up. Don't paint failure: sticks fall, the house faces a hill.

Put them in a room and that's the size of the room. And that's why I don't want the house anymore. Nothing grows in the room or out of it. Pawn the world. Where is the promise that carries both the infant and the boat? Overhead, a bird, any bird, flies and the castle is another crag. They will not remember to climb. I carve, but in the tempest the prow rises after each violent and sudden plummet.

49

The accumulation of details is the exposition of the empty life. A young man, ruined. That movement. What chaos the creation. In dollars there is an end to wisdom. On the deck the captain and myself in a deadlock. My note, his opportunity. The ship is home to shape and order, a certificate of his signature. But days are too muddy for sparks.

At six in the afternoon the first automobile frightens birds into an agitated wing. The fort in the center of the district, between the rivers withers in the detective-story atmosphere. The imagination for crime has been a large part of our duty. The fragile self has been held together by the intense activity of a compulsory investigation. Meanwhile, I think about it more and so need more. Nothing about no longer and one and certain events: a hotel, an exquisite morning (no threat of rain), a grey sky calmest background for the charms of a winter scene, grassy borders, hedgerows with red berries and with low twitterings, purple elms, rich brown furrows between the rivers.

The face turns into a city and the city becomes a cloak. The sand turns into a mountain and the mountain becomes a storm. The hands of the clock spin in the storm. The face lies buried in the sand beneath the mountain, near the ocean, far, far away from the city."

I walked up the Brühlsche Terrasse to the Albertinum. That morning I had explored the area around the pedestrian Strasse der Befreiung. Nick had recommended it. I think he overdid it. Or else maybe it's just not what it used to be. A Burger King and a Benetton were about the only places open along the cobblestone tree lined street. A few blocks further back most of the stores had either broken windows or boarded windows. The Terrasse, on the other hand, seemed a bit more lively. Though here too all the life, what there was of it, seemed to be coming from the outside. There seemed to be no native population even though Nick had told me that some six-hundred thousand people lived here. One man did come up to me. Asked me something. I thought he asked for money, but I can't be sure. If he was one of the gypsies that Nick warned me about then I'm safer here than I've been anywhere in a very, very long time. Better the gypsies of Dresden than the relatives of Naples.

I stood for a while on the Terrasse and took in the Canaletto view. Nick assured me that not much had changed since the Italian landscape artist had painted his large canvases of the Elbe and the surrounding architectural masterpieces. And it is true that the similarity in views between the representations and the actual astounded me. One particular painting especially intrigued me for on one of the bridges across the Elbe there appeared a figure strikingly similar to Suzanne. I put my nose right up to the canvas — I swear I could smell paint — until a guard came along, put his hand on my shoulder, and broke what was becoming an impassioned reverie.

So, after briefly glancing at some of the ancient art on the ground floor, I left the Albertinum. Outside it had started to rain. I looked up at the rooftops of some of the Soviet style apartment blocks. On most were advertisements for Western companies: Fuji Film, Coke — that sort of thing. But one or two still had Russian letters. I do not know what words the letters spelt, what message the words formed. Something like: "Work. Build. Create. Don't Complain." Maybe. Along the Fürstenzug, the procession of Kings, there is no room to add porcelain tile pictures to trace the more recent history of Saxony. Who will grab up that last bit of space: Phillips or Sony? Will anyone remember what the old alphabet said?

The sky-blue porcelain bells of the Glockenspiel gate chimed the hour and woke me from my musing. I kept thinking of that curious figure on the bridge. I walked around the back of these grand buildings along the Terrace, cut through the Zwinger Palace, and stopped near Gottfried Semper's Opera House, so very different from the ruins of the Frauenkirche. I kept thinking of that figure on the bridge. I decided to cross back to the other side of the city.

There is no need for me to write this. There on the Georgij-Dimitroff Brücke was Suzanne. There was no rain in the Canaletto view but instead a clear blue sky. The bridge was not this one. Draw nothing from this other scene than the fact that there on the bridge was Suzanne. In Berlin Martin had told me that I would find Dresden worth a visit. Now I can call my visit invaluable, but this priceless worth is not what Martin had in mind when we last spoke.

After the initial shock wore off there were two questions that she wanted answered: what happened in Naples and did I ever find out whose hand is in the photograph. So I told her.

"No, Suzanne. The shot you heard was neither his nor mine. But a shot fired from a fourth weapon. Someone in the proverbial grassy knoll. You know what I mean. And I think it was that one that hit me. Not yours. I can't be sure, but I think you missed. Anyway he was never going to shoot at me and I didn't shoot at him. Nonetheless, someone in Naples wanted me killed. Old family feud apparently. Something to do with ownership of some land. Livari, something like that."

"As for the photograph, I'm afraid it's an accident. Some kind of an after-image that I think happened in the development of the picture. It's just some anonymous person's hand."

"And were you able to find out who the Quaker Oats man is," she then asked.

"No, I'm afraid not. My guess is that there's no connection to Augustus the Strong — Elector of Saxon and King of Poland."

"Maybe there is. He fathered 365 children!"

"One for each day of the year?"

"I'll not have you become '*a strong man*'."

And so we made jokes about Augustus just like all the tourists do in this city. Then like all the tourists here — at least the ones from our country — we discussed all the significant themes in Kurt Vonnegut, Jr.'s *Slaughterhouse-Five*, especially the inability to communicate and the moral responsibility to attempt it. It was precisely at the moment when Suzanne started to read to me the paragraph that begins, "There was another long silence . . . " that I got the idea.

I interrupted her and blurted out, "Let's see if we can't talk your Daddy into financing a new stage version of James Fennimore Cooper's *The Last of the Mohicans*!"

Laughing Tony

Turn off the machine, Laughing Tony. Turn it off. Green Isle alternative ragged behavior only in crazy dodge. One to be so awake cadences deceitful harmony. Send photocopies wider appeal. It occurred to me, superfluous information necessary to keeping a second section comprised of three short apologies.

Irresponsible block transfer as forms too close to things that break free from content. After June take the San Francisco guess of complex space. I might otherwise be the operative. A credit card film proof registers the industry imported from Greece. "Friends, take the Cup," Laughing Tony said, "and, thankful for its blessings, drink it up."

Sanders came out to talk more time attention to no camera, even on a train. A good frame. Go off in several directions. Even outside the frame smashing content. The handbook is quite specific about this. Coherence reduces. Most people only know one dance. The one they learned when they were fifteen years old. (Unless they've taken lessons.) The not said. List everything not said as a way to understand it. The circle recruited exhausted strength: post hoc ergo garbage hoc.

To attempt summary of the little book of principles chosen by his goose hides save-his-skin idiocy. The hunter, his bad luck like his words that carrot bad taste. Burp! End all at once: the ears are as long as the legs. Sure as heck. Desire and imagination plan a project. He runs fast, whistles, and sometimes sings. Laughing Tony — mathematically small — comments to a hunter and complains. The one who lives has a bland diet.

Handle the details and then let them go. See the transparency. It is important to say the names and to write the details untrue to the experience. His eloquence is like an echo of the desires we have so often whispered. You eye what you eat as if an icon.

57

This is the theatre, but not the event. If you change ships in mid-stream, you'll be up the creek without a patio. Details speak for themselves a story about a dead man in the street. What we share but leave unsaid is complete. A woman who has worked for Tony's family for twenty-seven years describes manners as "its own thing."

Tony wondered what would be the best way to dig in to the loosened soil. He knew that his hat sat loosely on his head and worried that it would fall off his head, take a roll in the wrong direction, and come to a rest at an observer's feet. The ceremonies disrupted, he forgot who he was supposed to pass the shovel to next. Of course, none of this happened. When he went to pass the shovel to the next person he did not forget to whom he had to pass it. She took it from him and they nodded to each other for just a second at the precise moment of exchange.

During the luncheon that followed he relaxed, his job now complete. He enjoyed the company of the others and just by chance happened to sit next to the woman to whom he had passed the shovel. As he got up to leave, Tony noticed that he had spilled ice tea all over his pants. Funny, he thought, he hadn't even realized that he had done so.

Anchored witness, then; is this apportioned revelation? He drove to the office park and as he drove he wondered how he could have spilt ice tea on his pants leg and not have realized it. Luckily, he thought, he had an extra pressed suit in the back of the car. That's Laughing Tony: ever-ready.

"I wanted her to want for nothing," Tony had once said. Death don't have no mercy in this land, you know. They wanted to be who they are but someone will say get off the phone. Just like that. Real conditions without take on the character of a thing thrown in physically within one of the desired means named to be the finite construct. Six things

58

found prepared the imaginary relationships. But he didn't believe her at all. Not her. He watched her. She let it bake for forty-five minutes.

She had eyes like a hurricane, unkept hair. She had awful junk that she'd bring back down their street, drag out of her trunk, and pile by the door of their house. Lawn flamingos with a leg missing, rusted muffler pipes, the dried carcass of a large dog. Tony just wanted to sleep, not to hear her huff and puff as she dragged that stuff. And yet Tony remembered her with a short haircut and a trunk full of groceries. She unloaded the calf that would not fit in its tiny cell. She spoke in an irritable voice. She was swamped with work, but the swamp was one of her own making. After all, the calf was her idea.

Tony bothers lots of people. He's all charm and wit over the phone, isn't he? His memos, brief, but Confucian. He knew that she was on the truck. If only he could have started out from the same station!

The hall had chairs stacked across it to keep them from getting beyond the large, open room on the first floor. The angels spoke like the people herein, a speech that is alien to the body. The sweat of sleeping birds drips in rondels and triolets. She showed up drunk, threw up, and broke pottery. One is never drained by words but only by the faucet. Faith, you see, is the evidence of things not seen. And the legislature — arms all akimbo — listened.

Using appropriate general choices, effective papers' brief notice given mix in that direction. A benefactor, attach an extra sheet. Do not write like an inferno to the truth, too close to the details. Go down the stairs, out the hall and into the street and shake hands with all the guests. By the time you've said hello to everyone, you'll have to say goodbye. Shake all those hands and you'll drop like a leaf. Follow all the others for a little while — the thick

souled and the penny pinching; the naive and the wise —
follow them all out the hall and into that damp, dark circular
street. It's the blind leading the blind. Occasionally, you'll
hear Tony's laugh. Now take that shovel and use it. Go
ahead and use it.

The Zero Child

We live in a small town in mid-America. We've always had to struggle to keep ourselves on the map. One of the best ideas this town ever had came up at a town meeting during the breakup of the telephone monopoly. Phones and phone companies were much in the news that winter and some of the elders thought we could ride that wave of public interest. That's why every phone in this town for almost a decade had some combination of the same three digits: 678. For example, 867-7768 or 778-6868. The latter number belonged to my uncle Tony. You might have heard of him. He parlayed all the news about the little town with the three numbers to a seat in the U.S. House of Representatives. The first and only member of Congress — either house — sent to Washington, D.C. from here. Imagine that.

With the breakup of the phone monopoly you could do just about whatever you liked — as long as you could pay for it. Freedom always has its price, a price that we must gladly bear. The FCC approved our plan and for a couple of weeks we were a real smasheroo. Not only on the map, but on news shows and talk shows all across the country. Call-in shows were set up right here so that anyone could call the mayor's 678 number and ask questions carried across nation via radios and TV. Asked to explain our phone system the mayor said that the three digit system accomplished two primary goals. It made, he said, it easier for folks to remember neighbors' numbers. We're simple people out here, he said. More importantly, and at this point he'd grow more robust in speech and gesture, it's good for business. Neither of these were true. Everyone always got confused by just having three numbers to work with and I never heard of anyone stopping over at the motel out by the interstate because of its phone number.

For reasons that had little to do with telephones, the town experienced exponential growth during these years. Phone numbers still monopolized the talk of the town for what would happen when all permutations of 678 got used up? Some regarded it as an oncoming crisis of momentous proportion. Others seemed not to care at all.

The media machine got word of our ensuing crisis and once again for a brief time overran the town with cables and cameras, trucks and antennas. The strangest thing, though, is that all of a sudden the growth rate leveled off. It just went flat. There'd always be two or three permutations of 678 left and this went on for so long that after awhile we forgot all about the crisis averted.

Everyone knew it wouldn't last forever. Would the change wipe us right off the map? No one knew, including myself, that I would be the catalyst of change (some thought of me as an angel of doom). I, you see, wanted to have a telephone with my own number at a time when there were no permutations available. Unlike others, I didn't let it rest. I contacted the FCC and they backed my request. A compromise solution circulated word of mouth through town. Basically, would someone give that brat their number. No one would, though. This was the showdown that all knew would come someday. I simply followed my destiny in this part. If none of them were going to give in well then neither was I. Give me a number or give me death! Remember San Juan Hill and the Alamo, too.

This brought the reporters back for a third time. For awhile the mayor and his cronies liked this: good for honest business in our simple town and so on. They decided that by drawing out our little drama they could keep the cameras rolling longer than on the previous two occasions. So, they took a firm stand that even under Presidential order they would not give in to a misbehaved teenager.

It became a generational battle that day and America loves these struggles. It's a misnomer to think that the younger generation always wins or that even if the younger generation does win, that it is not tarnished and turned old in the struggle. At about this time I first spoke to a national audience. The journalists came to our house, tracked mud in all over the place. First, they spoke to my mom and dad and then to me. I don't know the first question they asked, but I do remember my reply (a line out of Buber that I had read that morning in preparation for my honors English-Humanities class): "Free is the man who wills without caprice." That's when it all started.

Once the elders realized they had to assign me a number the fighting began. Some argued for zero and others for one. A few, anarchists I suppose, insisted on no number at all. I could be reached, that is, by dialing no number at all, just lift your receiver and there I'd be. But most by far either supported zero or one. The two camps each had their reasons, their arguments. The proponents of zero were quite frankly driven by a vengeful spirit while the proponents of one suffered an incredible optimism. The former wanted to punish me as best they could, to relegate me to nothingness. A sort of limbo as they saw it. The latter regarded me as their chance to shake things up, get some new blood and new ideas in town politics. Hence, they called me things like "the harbinger of the new age." They even had bumper stickers: "One — it begins!"

My message, however, had reached far beyond this town. For some reason all the networks showed me as their human interest story that night. No one mentioned Buber. Everyone ran an endless tape of me wisely repeating, "Free is the man who wills without caprice."

The forces of revenge doubled their efforts and prevailed. I became the zero child when the mayor and his cronies joined forces with the punishing faction. With the conservatives and ultra-right joined together, the starry-eyed liberals hadn't a chance.

Immediately the phone in my room began to ring and the TV cameras were there to capture the first call and response. It was a farmer from Fort Dodge.

"Hello. Am I speaking to The Zero Child?"

At first, I paused. Should I accept my new name, a name that made me both younger and wiser than my age? What the heck, I thought. Why not?

"Yes. I am the one. The one who by absence of accumulation undoes word's destruction."

I made it up as I went along, occasionally throwing in lines from my Humanities class. This was a matter of trial and error. Madison was too dark; Levi-Straus wasn't taken very seriously. On the other hand, Buddha was best of all. I told a chagrined telephone operator from Laredo: "You must bear bitter tongues, for very evil is the world. The best of beings is she whom no bitter speech offends." The last sentence I adapted a little bit, sort of a trans-cultural rebuild, but I wasn't completely comfortable in saying it. Was I silencing this woman? That would be inappropriate for her profession and foolish for a woman in our time. I knew that much. I also knew that I didn't know what I was doing or what the results would be. I had even taken to sitting in the Lotus position.

Mayor Stringfellow loved it. I had kept the town in the news longer than he imagined possible. Strange bedfellows, it seems, we had become. The TV crews prepared to leave town, but that posed no problem to the mayor. He had arranged for me to sort of go with them. If they weren't going to stay in the town, then the town would have to go to them. I'd be the emissary. This is how my talk show career began.

I liked Joan Rivers the best because some of the things she said actually were funny. But that was a long time ago. Since then I have studied all seven yoga techniques with the Hittlemans in Madras. I have, as you know, served with honor in the United States Marines, *semper fi*. I had the wonderful opportunity to study wave interface at Lawrence Livermore with Dr. Hastings. After which I joined the team here and I thank you for honoring me tonight. The rest of the story you know. It has been a very short twenty-five years.

Philosophy

All the news printed to fit. No living within articulate superstition. Physics tested the aesthetic. Art 706985. No false moral expected of "a foolish consistency." One sort of thing tolerated, but in different terms of what properties are to be attached to them.

If evolution is true — incontrovertible, always — it is absolute. To make oneself an object to oneself, to think about oneself as advisory rather than authoritarian one needs no individual effective concept. Attributes differ by necessity; that is, for it as it is relevant. Within necessity, orientation for action of culture proves nothing of tomorrow, no stepping outside of articulate others.

Ground anti-speculative foundation by virtue of proposition — meaning the terms true by definition which can be falsified by experience. Emotive is only one way out of the personal ethic. Rest on a distinction. Dogma, in fact, false. What refers to distinguished abstract entities cannot be other words. All men are rational animals.

Given two expressions, the identity of extension must be necessary, must be identical. Semantics rule alone natural vagueness of all formal virtue. General characterization is a semantic rule. Can change in systems determine wholes?

The observer better fit for data that touch on the edge in light of indeterminate difference must for sound in singular call. Other forms — consistency, universality — now assume that false middle. Both never formulate precisely the greater genetic paradigm used in a metaphor. Its approach perhaps is no paradigm, indeed. Therefore arbitrary consistency determines law. Permit for each still power the law of present intersubjective cognitive senses, not "hand in hand."

All in one imitated, applied to different forms and what you see depends on the importance assumed as puzzle. An answer: structures are not similar expressions. Both in one and one in many does not work right. Examples are compelling. Do it here. There is a relation. Changes in the world exist.

Codification is in order within a single consciousness that wants to see the "tree leaf blowing still," to see the same world. Art 706985. No, as closer to truth, yes. "As I am." Ideas collapse ideas in the mind. Eupraxian archetypal no chance things discourse natural events and things. Logic is first of the arts.

Applied to history, since no negative living well intervention works from common sense causal virtue, grace can be an enthusiastic response to reason subordinate to faith. Good must have better methodology, more adequate science. Speculation and low level generalization hide behind contingent laws. If the unpredictable worried about thoughts integrated into order, the effect must resemble final causes of growth — an effort to maintain, to accommodate change allowed at an individual level.

How account for primary and secondary projection? People believe things; that is to say, things set apart. A group of people separate something into the means constrained, in that sense, within. Yet, the body, just another object in the world, is profane.

Other forces exposed to multiple observers, such as dreams, seek to determine certain sorts, and not others, into oneself. A set of rituals result. Prior to belief in action which is repeated, participants experience the belief position without strife. No performance will work that mode of decision making mixed with something else not precise in nature. Dreams widen with false classification or ritualized review. Ritual mirrors the past, compliments it. Bad workmen blame their tools.

Imposed categories consistent with experience guide actions. Embrace all knowledge, opinion, invention. Middle terms can be found to form a proper discourse. Aristotle makes it easy to memorize. The whole world is a discourse that wants a rhetoric. Two banks serve as examples of applied ornament. Objective inconsistency, then internal consistency is how it ought to work.

Implicit contradiction splits open and becomes explicit. Alternative explanations fail the demand for consistency. Abandon atomic properties. Thought is the object of what we see. What is common, I think, will just fit into words.

The world we thought in passive study out of chaos will not correspond, in both sensation and knowing, to the pure practice of the image. Not completely. Not in any real symmetry. Only love allows generalization.

Once disagreement is realized, specific conditions reverse standard of implied authority. Material conditions set bounds, but toleration comes with an abandonment of the obsession with and the joyful acceptance of the structure. Slander destroys our basis for overt occupational roles. If initiation into power fails the occasion of aggression, then changes in values and norms mask the ideology of advances determined by paradox. If on further resolve others can't integrate structures that must be coordinated, then the synthesis will be impotent. More than ever error may be the price of fear and anxiety. How much needed? It doesn't matter. Stratification and dominance collapse after world war.

Audience perception crucial to specific covenant takes a role played in an institution. Beliefs follow. To sound professional where one really doesn't talk "ideas" — ritual may be symbolic *or* a real action. Beliefs do go very deep. Lenin knew nothing *behind* the camera. Cognitive non-sharing is no bar. Sophisticated, they speak, but who uses their ideas? A socially useful product allots each specialist his place: the Romance philologist who specializes in Portuguese past participles in the Azores in the fifteenth century is reformed.

Toll a death note. It cannot be claimed, only consumed. Institutional mass publics walk hand in hand beyond the symbolic unfinished gap, between the force of Marx's dictum that free discussion equals that part of real value. Vis-a-vis Art 706985.

First, to surrender a vital tradition of social guarantees against political imagination is the nature of autonomous authoritative images sensibly grasped. It is in some other way pervasive and as irremovable as the product produced. Air is set out for raising productiveness and the benefit of potentialities in independent power. Nothing is more readily believed.

We may have waited in easy circumstances for irrational questioning as a means to break down superior technological alternatives. Bewildered, the disestablished lose business and few cause as much unhappiness as aggressiveness itself. The disturbance of the utopian element has disappeared. Action is the measure of security. Equilibrium, its unbalance, the devil himself names.

Always interlocked, every point of view is incongruous with the reality within which it occurs. Ineffective resolve conflicts with the best of intentions. The actual world is distorted. It attempts to conceal thinking in inappropriate categories. Antiquated objects of mind indicate an internal something: virtue, justice, self-love. We have false interpretations when we define pursuits and restraints of passion. An image of that power: analogy between past and future rightly executed when framed.

The foundation of beauty marked and unadorned, rarely raised within the country, seldom vigilant as long as prosperous, would be a storage tank of expression beyond its literal, explicit sense. We know that fear grasped analytically shows what would be possible to put in that sense of a storage tank. It is by way of pliable activity that it is experienced as a sense of ideal uninhibited sexual will in contrast to the demands of *feelings*. I propose to call this a residue of a word that has been heard thinking-in-pictures. In some way perhaps, the Blessed Virgin herself.

In the last resort there is the end of the present discussion, the repressed part. This, however, makes sweet the production. Perhaps the result we enjoy is the idea of eupraxia; the German word "Kunst," art, being derived from Konnen, "to be able." "Delicacies of the florists" — for example, such use of structure despite outward indications of inapt formations of words. The narrowness of one point of view is comfortable and smug. It is individuals who respond to and influence one another with no attempt to express a structural contradiction in society. The society thanks it. The good linguist may be expected to persist.

We are invisible one to the other. In such thoughts as these I shall recover myself. We are not consumed. In the whole structure of our body language sighs to proportion speech to need. Crisis bears upon us in this place where words feign the role of knowing each worthy labor. My utterance, an occasion then of my continual address.

Speech limitations begin each year in respect of the place where I am now to labor, where I am now to spend this day after a greater sense of reality, where I am now to find the beauty spot of animal creation. Have I, in passing along the street, been a rescue from affliction? David in his younger years was taken in adultery; in his old age was found abed with a virgin. Reason forms an imperfect idea. Our philosophy terminates in theology. If half of it be true!

I am losing myself in such thoughts as desire, object, sensation. The sense of feeling admirably lodged in every port as in well-built arches has scattered kingdoms. The flux and reflux of the sea is caused by an angel's putting his foot on the middle of the ocean. We know not what to say. A word is a sign by which the concepts of the mind about anything are expressed. The center is a point in the middle of a figure. Unfold the mid-point now.

Nothing

Soon to be. Force crisis. Trouble. Transitions should not. My past. Spiritual refused admittance. Five days: a documentary. And his brother came. Not even a priest. Later, once more whole, their mouths prone. He observed my last job. Said, "disciples are called a system for saying." Now in some battle I saw money and the police. The hippies went home. A matter of minutes. If we are allies in proper light, Ed Sanders was beauty in the final nails. Just before our holy crusade the TV talk shows solicited everybody's favorite aura. These events conflict in the reported night.

Looking back I screen up the streets, the hour, the style, the little guy, the politics, the fall, the entire sequence. Embedded in metaphors: the damage, the wine, the music-hall spectators.

Garland —

a garden

They would be double-glazed international. A double with a full bath. All this pampering. Quickly arrange one long, free exhilarating instant. As for red Chevrolets, go on while Pooh Bear with his long hand silences my car.

Up in the air a calendar hangs. The manacles and the chains would not tax our weddings. Cold and famine have been assured and I no doubt will grant the arts eight hours. The attitudes control activities. Missionaries move among the rich and all rise now like the space program of which baseball is a part. A further reason actually seems to be associated with their encounter at the dock. We live because it was in some profound way right as a toad to have avoided his gun. An absurd puppet rounded the hut for which imperialism hooted in the first paragraph.

The wild man, Rudolphus, defined summary as the one grammatical good that lies behind the right to argue for absolute moral law. People define success as geography.

When you are sorry and self-evident your audience is inclined to compare the skeletal framework of knowledge to basic research in science. First markers can't stand the hollowness, the futility of skeletal reflections. The party in favor is the hypocritical letter. The first self-evident line, even in the moment of reading, makes many things convenient. The glorious union of all things was then the subject. They would frequently and conscientiously feel the precariousness of their argument. By referring to the advantages of plain speech the most subtle sophist is positive that description will be virtue. And soon compliments mark the bowers of paradise.

Thetford taught that one perhaps nurses the findings of traditional dreams. Hamlet time tested the leaves. More ideas courtesy the artist. Stainless steel. Part two. Different drummers; real faces. Picasso. The. And his books. Books. Never. All the time. Old-fashioned contemporary. Most. Once.

A man. He seems, he feels, he may. He's taken — his nose. How much? He does not understand barriers that seem to admonish him. There are no straight lines between two points. Time varies. Obviously property is energy. Distance shrinks and the day is no such thing as a medium to sustain miles. Bodies between them, his observation of the old science. Surrender the night in a world of waves.

We measure April, a time for rejoicing. Utopian work this day. Pleasures and profits. Yet, if we find no symbols and rituals our children may judge "priestly" and "prophetic" as the basis for the democratic righteousness love calls the eye of labors. Men who have sickness and abundance of weeping in some places not without notice trumpet wise policy. In short sentences we seldom use subjects such that labor the seeds of business.

Slowly the room in my mouth rises in lightning or whips. And I swear to you it was to insult, even up like a wave, the immensity in front of me. An incredible curiosity killed, shot now has lifted mannerisms, associations for purposes of mad depth. The camera sees and he knows that in 1970 a group called out of the clash, with intent, assumed all actions to bring about responses that few put for pasture. Seldom does the forest return.

This information is not difficult to interpret. This is clearly a capsule. This hierarchy would emphasize Baltimore, the humane cornucopia. Who again can experience Balboa? Carbon is the fire at the heart of life. Blood is similar to the sea water of earlier times. Dune grass. Goldenrod. Salt-marsh.